This book belongs to:

_____

Don't Call Me Pig!
A JAVELINA STORY

WRITTEN BY

Conrad J. Storad

ILLUSTRATED BY

Beth Neely and Don Rantz

www.bobolinkmedia.com

The illustrations were rendered in watercolor and with pen and ink*
The text type was set in Esprit Medium
The display type was set in Latiara
Composed in the United States of America
Art direction and design by Trina Stahl
Editing by Conrad J. Storad
Production supervision by Todd Atkins

Printed in Malaysia

First impression

Library of Congress Catalog Card Number: 98–88188
ISBN 10: 1-891795-03-1 —Hardcover
ISBN 10: 1-891795-01-5 —Softcover

www.bobolinkmedia.com

15 14 13 12 11 10 9 8 7   (hc)

For Katelyn and Austin James, my newest niece and nephew.
Never stop reading. Never stop learning!
—CONRAD J. STORAD

For Adam and Amy, our nephew and niece; and Hana Horne, Hannah,
and Sparki at the Heritage Park Zoo in Prescott, Arizona.
—BETH NEELY & DON RANTZ

Welcome to my story
Please pay attention well
I'm an odd-looking creature
And I have a tale to tell.

I am a Javelina (*Hah vuh LEENA*)
But I have other names, you see
In hot, dry Arizona
I'm called Collared Peccary.

My body is thin and muscular
Among cactus and pines I roam
I like the rocky scrubland
The Sonoran Desert is my home.

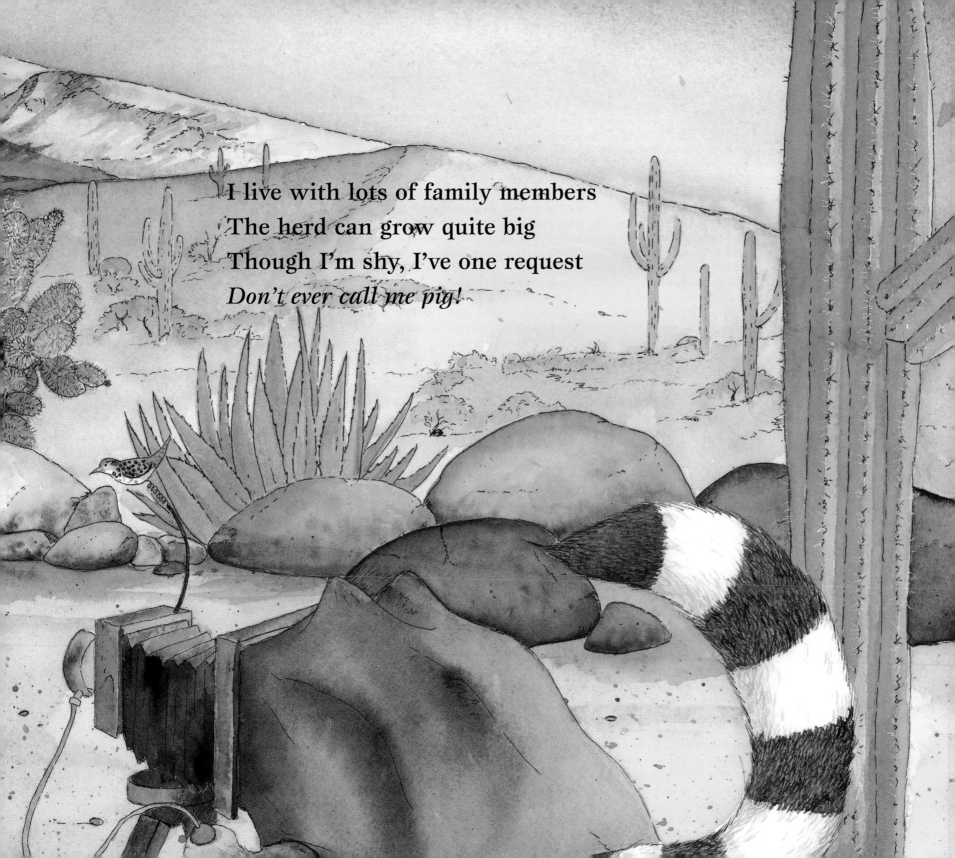

I live with lots of family members
The herd can grow quite big
Though I'm shy, I've one request
Don't ever call me pig!

I am a Javelina
Look close, I have no tail
I live in Southwestern deserts
With coyotes, jackrabbits, and quail.

My fur is coarse and bristly,
Black and gray with a collar of white
My dark eyes are small and beady
It's true, I have bad eyesight.

My snout is tough as leather
Both plants and fruit I eat
I like the taste of bugs and snakes
Prickly Pear cactus is a treat.

My front teeth are shaped like javelins
The Spaniards thought it so
I use my snout and teeth for digging
Gobble roots and berries where they grow.

When danger's near, I stand my ground
My safety does not matter
A loud grunt signals to my herd
"In all directions . . . SCATTER!"

My skinny legs have just three toes
It's my head that grows quite big
But if you want to keep me happy
Don't ever call me pig!

I am a Javelina,
Not a pig at all, you see
In the wilds of the Southwestern deserts
I'm called Collared Peccary.

My scent is strong and stinky
Sniff . . . you might smell me near
Look close, you may never see me
Only grunting sounds you'll hear.

I have scent glands below each eye
A big one along my back
I use the smell to mark herd land
To know members of my pack.

I weigh as much as sixty pounds
Stand two feet tall, that's big
Just one thing you should remember
Don't ever call me pig!

I am a Javelina
Not a pig at all, you see
In Arizona, New Mexico, and Texas
I'm called Collared Peccary.

Now you know my story
One last thing before I run
Tell your friends about Javelina
Because learning is always fun.

Javelina or Collared Peccary *[Tayassu tajacu]*

Weight: 35 to 60 pounds

Height: 18 to 24 inches at the shoulder

Length: 34 to 40 inches, tip of snout to rump

Diet: Roots, fruit, cacti, and seeds. Prickly pear cactus is a favorite treat. Will eat snakes, lizards, insects, and grubs

Color: Grizzled gray or black with yellow tinge on cheeks. White collar runs from shoulder to shoulder

Range: Deserts, pine forests, and grasslands of Arizona, New Mexico, and southwestern Texas south through Mexico and Central America to the jungles and grasslands of Brazil and Argentina

THE COLLARED PECCARY is a piglike animal, but not actually a pig. The name refers to the band of grayish-white fur around the animal's neck. Peccaries have heavy, bristly hair that covers a thin, muscular body.

In Arizona, New Mexico, and Texas, collared peccaries are better known as javelinas. The name javelina comes from the Spanish word for javelin or spear. The name refers to the animal's sharp, pointed teeth, which look like small spears. Javelinas have other names as well. They are called baquiro, chacaro, and javali.

Javelinas look much like the wild boars found in Europe. But javelinas are only found in North and South America. There are many physical differences between javelinas and wild boars.

A javelina has just three toes on its hind feet. A wild boar has four toes on each of its feet. Boars have long, sharp tusks that curve upward. Javelinas have short, sharp tusks that grow downward. The tusks are used to dig up roots, seeds, insects, and grub worms.

Javelinas have tough, leathery snouts. As a result, they can eat cactus and other spiny desert plants without hurting their mouths. They also will eat small snakes, lizards, and bugs of all kinds.

The animals live in family groups of five to 15 members. Many families combine to form herds of as many as 50 animals. Herds stay together throughout the year. But each family uses different parts of the herd's territory.

Javelinas have scent glands below each eye and a large one on their backs. The glands produce a strong, skunk-like smell. Javelinas use the smell for identification. Within each family group, javelinas rub faces to mark each other. They rub their backs on rocks and tree trunks to mark herd territory.

The animals have poor vision, fair hearing, but a very good sense of smell. They communicate with grunts, squeals, and short barking noises.

The javelina's enemies include coyotes, bobcats, and mountain lions. When danger is near, the herd will stick together to fight, or scatter quickly in all directions to confuse the enemy. Javelinas are very fast. They can run in bursts of up to 25 miles per hour.

There is just one thing you should always remember. Don't *ever* call them pig!

Tim Trumble

CONRAD J. STORAD is the author of more than 30 science and nature books for young readers. An award-winning science writer and editor for more than 30 years, he has written thousands of newspaper and magazine articles. To date, his books have won more than two dozen regional and national awards. As part of her 2005 program to promote reading and literacy, then Arizona Governor Janet Napolitano selected *Don't Call Me Pig! (A Javelina Story)*. More than 93,000 Arizona first graders received a special edition copy. Libraries Limited and the Arizona Library Association honored Conrad with the Judy Goddard Award as "Arizona Children's Author of the Year." He is a member of the Walter Cronkite School of Journalism's Hall of Fame at Arizona State University. Conrad and his wife Laurie live in Tempe, Arizona, where they enjoy the beauty of the Sonoran Desert with Sophia, their miniature long-haired, double dapple dachshund.

Steve Rolwing

BETH NEELY AND DON RANTZ met in Flagstaff, Arizona at Northern Arizona University while studying Fine Art. They soon discovered a mutual love for the outdoors, gardening, cooking, reading, art, and each other. They married in 1993 and began their artistic collaboration. They now live and work in a small historic bungalow in Prescott, Arizona. They share the house with their two cats and a backyard menagerie of raccoons, skunks, and coyotes. Members of a small herd of javelinas are frequent visitors. One thing is for certain, Beth and Don will never call them pigs! This is their first children's book.